The Lift

by

Andrew Barrett

© Copyright 2015
Andrew Barrett

The rights of Andrew Barrett to be identified as the author of this work have been asserted in accordance with sections 77 and 78 of the Copyright, Designs and Patents Act 1988. No part of this publication may be reproduced, stored in a retrieval system or transmitted in any form or by any means electronic, mechanical, photocopying, recording or otherwise without the prior permission of the copyright holder

All characters and events in this publication are fictitious, and any resemblance is purely coincidental.

For

Sarah

The Lift

Today, two events changed my life.

They didn't make me turn to religion or become a vegetarian, nothing quite so drastic; but for me they had a profound effect, like a stutter in life's journey – a hesitant footstep from one predictable day to the next.

I've seen scores of bodies in my time, and they don't bother me as long as they're not slimy, maggoty, or too smelly; certainly nothing to put me off my Big Mac. But for the first time ever, today I saw a live person become a dead person. There was no ethereal moment where I saw the soul rise from the warm corpse, nothing quite so dramatic. Just the final exhale and then over a period of a minute or two, the eyes began to cloud over.

At exactly the same moment as the person became a corpse I witnessed the second event. I saw a person become a killer. As the corpse's eyes milked over, this guy's eyes turned feral. Now *that* would put me off my burger. That was fucking frightening.

I flicked away my cigarette and stared at the butt ugly tower block and its cloned brethren. Depressing. Why do they do that, the architects, why do they go out of their way to make something depressing to exist in? I could have done better with some Lego blocks and a tube of UHU. The whole estate was like a prison, and I bet that's how it felt to live there.

I ignored the graffiti surrounding the intercom panel, buzzed flat 68 and waited for a reply. It didn't arrive and I sighed again. It was going to be another shit day. I'd been in the office for precisely eight minutes; just long enough to grab a radio and battery, my kit and van keys, and have a brief altercation with my arsehole of a boss.

It wasn't my fault. He was grumbling about my paperwork not being up to date, about statements I needed to do. We slipped back into the same old argument, the same old rut; it was like being married to a monotonous fat prick who only knew how to highlight problems and didn't have a Scooby how to fix them. The way I see it, my job is out here catching the scrotes who made people's lives even more miserable than the architects were doing, not sitting behind a desk writing statements for the courts to play with. I know, I know, it's part of my job and it's what I signed up for all those years ago, but writing a statement can take two or sometimes three hours. I could have attended three burglary scenes in that time, or a rape scene, or a fire scene. In short, I could have helped the people who needed it instead of fucking about helping some barrister pay for his next yacht. You think all criminals wear gloves and a mask? Nope, there are quite a few who wear gowns and wigs too.

Anyway, I'd gathered my gear together, letting his ranting fall out of my brain as though it were a party political broadcast, and marched out of the office, telling him to get a clerical assistant to write the damned statements. I'm pretty sure the stapler missed my head by less than an inch but I didn't care, I was out of there. Happy days.

Sort of. And now, as I lit another cigarette and leaned against the entrance waiting for someone to let me in, I wondered what kind of person could talk their way into an elderly person's flat and rob them blind. They usually pretended to be from the water company, asking them to check under the kitchen sink and when they did, the bogus official – the bogoff – would nip into the bedroom and steal a wallet or a purse. They didn't care about the carnage they left behind. I remember one bogoff where they took everything, the old guy's medals, his change, even his bus pass. I can still see his crumpled face to this day, and if I'm on a real downer, it can make me weep.

These bastards didn't have a conscience, that was for sure, but they had balls. Either way I'd love to get my hands on one of them for ten minutes – it'd be enough to convince them never to do it again. And when I say I'd like to get my hands on them for ten minutes, I mean I'd like to get my hands on *them*, not their balls. That thought tickled me and I found myself smiling a bit, secretively like I was being naughty, when they walked into view.

I continued to smoke even though I'd bludgeoned the smile to death, and watched them, a young scrote in a freshly stolen tracksuit, and an old guy; his grandfather maybe? Scrotes don't like it when you watch them; staring at them makes them feel self-conscious, and if they're up to no good – which most folk their age around here are – they get nervous, even though this kid seemed nervous to begin with, almost pleading with his grandfather who shoved him in the back every few paces, still unfortunately out of range for me to listen to.

Seeing me in my uniform, black jacket with reflective blue and white tape, black trousers, heavy black boots, a never silent radio clipped to a shoulder harness, a very long and very heavy Maglite dangling from a loop on my belt, shut the kid up quick. When they saw me, they almost came to a stop and I could tell they'd considered just turning around and walking away by the way they glanced at each other. The scrote mumbled something and the old fella kind of growled, and they began walking again, but there was a definite reluctance in their gait and a silent curse on their lips.

By this time, I suppose it was too late to stop and turn around; they were nearly here, and walking off now would've been very suspicious indeed. You see, they dress us like coppers. A quick glance at me and you'd mistake me for one, yet I have no more powers of arrest than you do. I'm a toothless tiger, a pencil with no lead; whatever. If it was the Authority's aim to make the streets appear more heavily populated with police officers by dressing me up in their party clothes, then it worked.

The scrote looked at the floor for the final few steps before they both stood at my side. One of them, probably the youth, stank like week-old sweat. It was nauseating. The old fella looked at the youth and growled, "Do it." The kid tutted, pressed a buzzer, and then pressed a whole row of buzzers. They looked away from me as they waited, the old guy clearing his throat as though he was about to speak, but changed his mind.

I didn't look away. I smoked my cigarette and I stared at the youth with his ear studs, his bum-fluff moustache, and his downcast dark eyes. The old fella wore a pristine blue shirt and tie, grey slacks and, surprisingly, white trainers. His eyes were pale blue, and he stood out for me, other than the trainers/tie combo, because of his greasy yellow hair which complemented his bushy moustache with a chain-smoker's yellow stripe running up through its centre. His fingers were similarly nicotine stained. I couldn't take my eyes off either of them.

Now you might think I was being intentionally intimidating; that I was guilty of prejudice, that I should give each person a chance based on their actions and demeanour, that I shouldn't judge people. Bollocks. Yes, I was being intentionally intimidating because I could imagine how many youngsters playing on the swings the youth here had intimidated, how many mothers pushing prams away from school he'd sneered at or leered at, or how many old people avoided the local Post Office because of pricks like him belittling them. I nurtured a kind of respect for the old guy because it felt good to see that some kids were still kept on a short leash. And then I wondered why the kid was on a short leash? What had he done in order for Granddad to be in on the act?

A crackly high-pitched voice came back over the intercom, and the youth said, "Yo, 'smee."

I nearly spat out my cigarette. 'Yo, 'smee'? What was all that about?

There came a grunt, followed by several more grunts, several more people in flats up and down the block either answering the buzzer or just activating the door release irrespective of who it might be out here waiting to get in. Either way, the lock clicked and the youth was through the door and into the echo chamber of the foyer, designer trainers squeaking on the smooth painted floor. The old man followed close behind, his back straight as a slab of concrete and nicotine moustache leading the way as though sniffing out a rat – or a turd. At that moment, as I flicked away my cigarette, loaded the camera bag onto my shoulder and grabbed my forensic kit, the lift doors trundled slowly open and an old lady wearing a black beany hat and carrying one of those bags for life teetered out on pins that had seen better days. She seemingly ignored the old fella, saw only the youth, and I could tell she was a little startled, but she did what most elderly people do, she kept herself on full alert and focused somewhere in the mid-distance. That somewhere was me. And I held the door for her. The youth boarded the lift and was less than polite to the old lady, affording her little room, and I heard the old guy snap, "Grant!"

The kid's disrespect made my hackles rise and I smiled an apology at her, swung the door wide and she, bless her, quickened her stride. "No rush," I said, "take your time."

I could see the youth, this Grant kid in the lift, turn around to face me, a very slight twinkle in his eye as though he'd got one over on me. Granddad was in the lift beating the button inside with a jack hammer. Whatever happened to waiting for me!

The old lady didn't so much as look at me as she exited the building, not so much as a smile or a thanks for holding the door open. "You're welcome," I said as she ambled past. "No really, don't mention it." Old cow still ignored me. "Oh. You didn't." Some old people don't fit into the stereotypical mould you just created for them.

Just as some youths don't, right? And just like Grant's granddad wasn't prepared to wait for me despite my display of gallantry to the old girl, and despite me carrying a shitload of bags and equipment.

Okay, point conceded.

Anyway, the lift door was closing just as I reached it. I stuck a boot in the decreasing gap and the doors shuddered and then opened again. I stepped aboard and eyed them both. The youth appeared more nervous than ever, and his shoulders slumped a little. I wondered later, if that little twinkle in his eye was something far more watery. This was going to be an interesting ride.

No one spoke.

The doors trundled shut behind me and I put my forensic kit on the floor, hitched the camera bag further up my shoulder and stared this time at the stainless steel walls. They were nobbly. I mean they weren't flat, the walls, they were pressed so there were bobbles in regular patterns all over them. This was my favourite type of lift wall. Yes, I know how weird that sounds but stay with me; they were the type that you could see on many different focal points. Remember those books that were all the rage ten years ago, the ones that looked like miscellaneous shapes until you stared *through* them, until you focused on a level below them, and then suddenly the miscellaneous patterns made sense? Well, these bobbles didn't make any more sense, they were still just bobbles, but you could see them one, two and sometimes three levels below their true distance. I'm smiling here because I know you haven't got a clue what I'm on about. But it's a good way to pass the time when you're travelling in a lift.

On the grey tiled floor were blackened spots of discarded chewing gum. The ceiling had graffiti on it, and overall the lift smelled faintly of disinfectant. I say faintly because it also smelled of piss, and the piss was winning hands down. Along with the recently introduced stench of body odour, I imagined the disinfectant would be making a grab for the white flag any time soon.

Still no one spoke.

There was more graffiti, obscene this time, scratched into the walls, and I wondered how they'd got away with it considering the camera was supposedly watching, and I also wondered what the arseholes who did it got out of it. Why would you want to scratch a penis on a lift wall?

At least I didn't feel claustrophobic like I do in some of the smaller lifts; this was maybe five feet square so at least there was breathing room. I've been in some that wouldn't even take three people, and if you're one of the two people in it, you couldn't avoid invading their space – horrid.

As we ascended, I could hear the machinery struggling to haul us upwards, could hear the cables whipping in the shaft, and as I turned around, I saw the brickwork between the floors drifting downwards through the cracked, wire-reinforced window in the door. Above my head, a camera peeking out from a little stainless steel nest recorded our joviality. And over the door, red digital numbers, some of their elements missing, ticked off the floors very slowly.

I looked back at the youth and he was studying the red digits too. Maybe it was the first time he'd actually counted without using his fingers. This lift, it seemed, was providing a valuable public service.

I studied the unlikely pair and couldn't quite work out their dynamic. "You related?"

The youth was about to speak, but the old guy cut him dead, "Nah," he said, "we're just good friends."

"But—"

"Isn't that right? Grant?"

Grant said nothing, stared at the floor, and the old guy stared at me with a false smile on his lips as if to say, 'Satisfied?' Well, I wasn't. There was something strange about them, and I wondered if that something strange was sexual. Good friends, eh?

The youth was itchy, antsy, call it whatever you want, but two things were obvious to me: he didn't want to be with his 'good friend', and he didn't want to be here in this lift heading to wherever he was heading. He felt uncomfortable, uneasy to the point of screaming, feet tapping out a tune maybe or just moving because he had too much nervous energy thrumming around his system. Was it nerves, I wondered, or was it drugs? His eyes looked dull, not fully opened, as though he'd only just woken up, yet their pupils seemed a normal size. His right hand rattled loose change in his pocket, his left drummed against the lift wall in rhythm with his foot. If I said 'boo', he'd likely have a heart attack and drop dead on the spot.

I was tempted.

The old guy was quite different. His eyes wandered only occasionally; his red complexion gave him a healthy country look that complemented his big rough hands. But his whole ensemble was a little skew-whiff with the out of date suit he wore. I wondered if he were ex-military such was his upright stance and his overall demeanour. The only thing that threw me off his scent were the trainers. Weird.

He was silent, still, his fingers didn't twitch, his feet didn't tap out a beat, he didn't silently whistle a tune, he didn't even find the lift walls entertaining. His eyes became still as though inside he was pondering something.

And I believe that something was me.

Eventually, the old fella's gaze dropped to the unmarked black kit box then flicked up to the Nikon bag. And finally his eyes settled on my radio. During normal use the radio has a pretty green flashing LED mounted on top and the screen illuminates when there's a transmission in progress. Right now though, the LED was a steady red. No signal. Screen unlit.

I could tell he had business to attend to, and he ached to be free of this lift and of me. There was a weird kind of crackling in the air, a tension that I didn't much care for yet wasn't afraid of; it was my kind of thing where the heartbeat is raised slightly and your hands had become fists without you even knowing. It was a tolerance, a live and let live standoff that only a short journey permitted. They kept sneaking glances at me, and looked away quickly each time I met their eyes with a glare of my own. It was amusing until eventually the old guy didn't look away.

And then things went wrong.

The old motor hauling me, an old guy, and a piece of trash up the insides of a decaying joke, shuddered, screamed, and then finally stopped. It was like a mechanical heart attack.

"Fuck," Grant yelped.

"Mind your language, boy." The old guy said. "What happened?"

They both eyed me as though it was my fault. I looked through the tiny cracked window in the door and noted the bricks were completely stationary. Bollocks, I thought.

I'd been right, this was going to be a shit day. As well as being cooped up with a moron and a pensioner, I would be forced to engage in conversation with them. I shrugged, "It's a wild guess, but I'd say the lift has stopped."

They appeared confused, trying to decide if that answer was sufficiently comprehensive.

"So what you gonna do, man?"

I slipped the camera bag off my shoulder and dropped it by my kit bag, relieved to give my aching shoulder a break, and took out my mobile phone. I'm not one for phones really, on account of I don't like talking to people so it seemed a waste of money having one. But they're good for other things too. You can play games on them; no not your Grand Theft Auto type games, which are for hermits and people of limited intelligence. No, I bought a mobile phone for the board games and the other more interesting things they could do.

"No signal in here, mate," Grant mumbled.

"I don't care. I'm playing Spider Solitaire. Now if you'll excuse me." I tapped my mobile phone's screen a few times, activating an app but making sure neither of them could see what I was doing. I then scrolled through the various screens until I found solitaire.

"What? We're stuck in a lift and you're playing fucking card games?"

"I said mind your language." The old man turned to the youth, who was almost as tall as him, and growled like a pit bull. The kid shrank back into a corner, glancing at me for some kind of support.

If I hadn't been stuck in a lift, I would have laughed. I was kind of warming to the old guy; he had character, and he wasn't boring. There seemed to be no stereotype he fell easily into, thanks to his trainers I suppose. But this guy was utterly without cliché.

I found myself staring at him, intrigued by his moustache and his sharp, mean little eyes. And then his demeanour seemed to change. He smiled at me. "I'm Reg," he said. "Reg Harding."

Inside my head, I screamed, please don't hold out your hand, please don't hold out—and then he held out his fucking hand. I looked at it, and thought it just too rude not to swap the phone to my other hand and shake. He smiled wider, and I felt dirty. The warmth I had for him only a few moments ago, dissipated pretty quickly. I also saw he was expecting a name; it was customary apparently, though I didn't really see why I should oblige. But still, here we were, three strangers locked up in a metal box. And who knew how long for. Could be hours, and although I wasn't bothered about those two getting on each other's tits, I wasn't so keen on being the outsider. It was more prudent to be liked right now. Reg was no streak of piss and the wrinkles and yellow hair belied a sturdy physique. "Eddie Collins," I said.

"I'm Grant," the youth announced.

Reg spun on his heels. "You just keep your dirty little mouth shut, boy."

Grant looked nonplussed, didn't even swallow, but when Reg took a small step towards him, he practically shat himself, hands out, placid smile on his face, wide eyes and exposed throat. "Okay, man, okay."

"That's better," Reg said, and turned back to me.

And then Grant said, "What about your radio?"

Now I wasn't sure if he was being brave or stupid. I saw no reason for him to antagonise Reg by not keeping his dirty little mouth shut, so I figured he was just stupid. Either way, I didn't want the temperature in here to rise, so before Reg could growl at the kid again, I said, "No signal," and angled the radio towards them as if in confirmation. "Why don't you see if the panel has an alarm button?"

It did, and Grant gave it a solid push with his thumb. We couldn't hear anything new, no buzzer, no bells or klaxon. He pushed again, and then punched the wall, "I gotta get out of here!"

"Late for your jog?" I asked.

"Come on man, do something."

"Keep your mouth shut." Reg said with some force, and now any feelings I had towards him were edging away from like and into dislike territory, with a healthy dose of caution thrown in for good measure.

"Quiet," I smiled at them both, "I'm on a winning run here." My joviality had no effect at all.

"Fucking piece of shit!" Grant kicked the lift wall.

"Oi, calm it." I said quickly, hoping to get in before Reg did his pit bull impression again.

"Piece of shit!"

"Yes, you already said that."

"No law against it, is there?"

"The Anti-repetition Act 1996," I said.

Grant looked confused. "Really?"

Thankfully Reg took a step back and laughed, "He's pulling your pisser, boy."

It felt like hours, but it had probably only been about seven minutes since my last cigarette. I could really do with another. I even thought of offering them around, since I guessed Grant smoked and I could even see Reg's packet of Richmond's poking out of his shirt pocket. But it seemed wrong. Not because of the camera peering over my shoulder, but because if the lift were to start up again in a minute and some old dear got in next... Well, it just didn't seem right.

Reg's eyes were locked on my uniform. On the left breast I wear a badge that says Police Staff. "You a SOCO?"

I nodded, "They call us CSI these days."

"What you here for?" This was from Grant who seemed smaller somehow, melded into the corner.

"I'm setting up covert obs on a bank robber."

He was about to say 'really' again, when Reg laughed, "He's not allowed to say, idiot."

Grant deflated and looked away.

"But," Reg went on, "I'd guess you're heading for 68."

I looked at him. Now I *really* didn't like him.

"Bogoff?"

I asked, "Is that where you're going?"

"My sister's flat," he said.

"It weren't me."

Reg moved to strike him and the kid reacted so fast that he smacked his head against the wall. Reg had only moved a few inches, backhand at the ready, no intention of connecting, but it was enough to shut the kid up.

"Enough of that, eh?" I stared at Reg and the old fuck stared right back at me.

And then his face relaxed, "Fair enough," he smiled. "Just having a laugh. And for the record, he *did* do it. The little bastard."

"I never," Grant mumbled.

"Can't fool me," Reg stuck out his chest. "Ex-copper. Leeds City Police." He obviously expected some reaction, a pat on the back maybe, a thumbs up, a professional nod of the head. He got nothing. "1976, Millgarth. You ever been inside Millgarth?"

I had many times, and I nodded. It was the kind of building you couldn't wait to get out of. It reeked of oppression. It seemed full of ghosts of old coppers swaggering about pissed in tweed sports jackets or rolled up shirt sleeves, fags dangling from their lips, pens behind ears, knuckles red or bruised. Indeed the place still smelled of old cigarettes and there were still ashtrays in the lifts. Not that you were allowed to use them now.

And I didn't doubt for a second that Reg was telling the truth. He was the cliché I'd been searching for. The kind of copper that got results by being brutal. Didn't matter if they were the right results or not. He was the kind of old school copper that abused the system so badly that the government created and introduced the Police and Criminal Evidence Act. Reg's own knuckles were so big and calloused that I assumed he had to have his knuckle dusters specially made.

"Twenty-five years," he said, grinning like I gave a shit.

"Congratulations, you must be very proud." I knew as soon as I'd mumbled it, and as soon as the sickly grin shrivelled under his yellow moustache, that I'd offended dear old Reg. I tried to mend the bridges again, but his face had soured considerably. "Get a Long Service medal?"

"It might not mean much to you, kid," he glared at me, "but coppering back in them days was bloody hard graft; proper police work, not sat by a bleeding computer like they do now."

All I had to do was mention one name and I knew I could deck his false modesty: Sutcliffe. But I chose not to, seeing as we were all trapped inside a steel coffin with pretty walls. And besides, I kind of saw the point he was trying to make. It must have appeared to him as though modern police work was inferior to the type of work it had been back then. I suppose demeaning women, inventing new names for black people, and beating the shit out of some random guy pulled in off the street without spilling your beer, *was* bloody hard work. And then, as if things weren't quite bad enough, Grant decided to chip in.

"Did you get to drive them old Granadas?"

"Aye."

Grant was smiling. This was possibly an error. "Through cardboard boxes." And then he laughed – definitely an error; the cardboard boxes thing was supposed to be a reference to old cop shows like *The Sweeney*, but Reg was nothing if not proud of his history, and the backhand deftly delivered across Grant's right cheek soon stopped him smiling.

Although I guessed him to be in his twenties, Grant stared at me over a hand that was curled around the redness of his cheek and his throbbing lip, and tears grew in his eyes like leaking taps. All this happened within the space of only a few seconds, and in that few seconds I went from being reasonably comfortable with my position in that steel coffin, to feeling vulnerable, the piggy in the middle, to feeling like this fucking curse of a uniform they'd given me somehow entitled Grant to justice, or at least protection, and somehow suggested I should mediate this situation.

Fuck the old lady, I put my phone down and lit a cigarette.

I breathed smoke upwards, and tried to fulfil my newly designated role as UN Peacekeeper. "You," I nodded at Grant, "would be wise to shut the fuck up." The taps dripped some more. "And you—"

"Don't give me none of your bullshit. That badge means nothing to me. Got it?"

I did get it. Very well, thank you. "Calm down, Reg. We might be in here for another ten hours and I'm telling you right now, I'm not playing referee to you two."

For some reason, that made Reg smile. "We don't need no referee."

"You will when we get out of here." I held his gaze. I usually loved intimidating people, did it for a sport. But now I was doing it to preserve the pecking order. If it worked, everything would return to simmer, if it didn't, Reg would likely relive some of his old coppering days. If I hadn't been stuck inside this lift, I would have gladly opened the door and walked away, leaving them to it. That's a shit thing to say, but my role in life is to find criminals after the event, not watching them create the event. And yes, I was nervous. Reg was not so much a loose cannon, he was plain fucking nuts. And everyone I've ever come across who was plain fucking nuts was a person you could not reason with on anything other than a shallow level, such as the weather or the football results. Once the bear's out of the cage, he's never going back inside it.

I still stared.

He looked away first, and I hastily swallowed the bucketful of saliva that had collected in my mouth, but maintained the stare for when he returned his own gaze, complete with smile.

He nodded, "Fair enough."

"I want to put in a complaint."

I closed my eyes and took a huge swallow on my cigarette.

"He just hit me. You saw him do it." Grant stared through his running taps right at me. "You saw him," he said again.

I wanted to scream at these two arseholes that all I did was spread fingerprint powder around people's houses. Aside from any street sense I'd picked up along the way, I had sod all training in how to keep the peace.

"And when we get to 68," Reg said, "you'll have something else to complain about."

"I didn't do anything!"

Reg was unimpressed by the vehemence of Grant's protests. "Really?"

"Your sister won't even recognise me. It's the only reason I came along. You haven't got shit all on me, man."

"You came along because I fucking dragged you, let's get that clear. And let's get this clear too: you did it, I *know* you did it. A copper never loses his sense of smell, and right now I smell a scrote, kid."

I'd read the log and I knew there was no way she could know it was him. "So what happens if your sister *doesn't* recognise him?"

Reg took a step towards me, and I don't mind admitting that I wanted to take a step back. But there was a steel wall in the way, so I did what I could to preserve that delicate pecking order – I took a step towards him, eyebrows raised in some unspoken challenge, like a taunt, something that said 'You wanna try your luck?'.

Reg placed his hand gently on my shoulder. And squeezed. Eyes drilling into mine. "He did it. My sister will *say* he did it."

"You see?" Grant cleared his throat and any of the emotion he'd recently shown had vanished. It was as if he'd resigned himself to his fate and was steeling himself in preparation for it. "Old coppers never die; they just get twisted."

Reg's face grew red and he let go of my shoulder. He turned to face Grant, but stopped moving because of the blade at his throat.

Shit. I dropped my cigarette and stood on it, glanced at the LED on my radio – still red. And through the little window in the door the bricks were stationary. Fuck, I did not need this. The tension in that small lift had ramped up to intolerable. Writing statements seemed like a great proposition just now. Apart from Reg's imminent death, all I could think of was my boss asking why I didn't prevent a stabbing. But what could I do? Really?

"Take it easy, kid," Reg said. "No need for this."

"Like fuck there is. I'll be a bleeding pulp when you've finished with me."

Reg slowly turned his body, blade scraping across the loose wrinkled skin of his neck. The kid didn't take the blade away, held it out at full arm's length, its tip slicing a neat cut and leaving behind a narrow crimson streak that developed into a curtain, and with each degree Reg turned, Grant's bravery was tested. He did well, but his arm began to shake, his bravery collapsing slowly. "You just crossed a line."

"There was never a fucking line, you old prick. I was always gonna be the sludge you scraped from under your finger nails when this day was over with. I thought once your sister had ruled me out, you'd see sense and let me go, like. But I'm your feel-good factor. I'm the one who's gonna make you look good."

"Shut it, kid."

The knife dug a little deeper, but rather than shy away from it, Reg gritted his teeth and moved into it. "You spineless little fuck; robbing old ladies, but with no balls to take the punishment. Happy to spend their pension but no too keen when it comes to payback, are we?"

"She can't possibly pick me out."

"Why?" I said wondering if my dream of spending ten minutes with a bogoff was actually here.

"She, she just can't!"

"Why!" Reg screamed.

"It wasn't me, that's why."

"Lying little shit. Tell me why you think she can't pick you out."

"Fuck off." His bravery waned further.

"Tell me!"

"Cos she's blind as a fucking bat!" Grant's eyes widened slightly, and then his entire face sagged. "Oh fuck," he whispered. The knife fell to his side.

"And how do you know that?" Reg asked. "How do you know she's blind?"

Grant swallowed, and his face begging for mercy.

Reg scraped at the blood on his neck, leaving a smear right along his forearm. "Her name is Shirley. She's eighty-six. She's lived through the war, was blinded by it in a munitions factory accident. And even after the war, she still had her fair share of bad luck. Her husband died five years ago, so now she's all alone on the tenth floor of a shithole slum like this.

"But that's not quite bad enough. Is it, Grant? You obviously thought her life was still too good, still too fucking easy! Because your life is far worse than hers, isn't it. Isn't it!" Grant said nothing. "No, she's too trusting. Opened the door to you and you took her cash, and you took her husband's medals. Did you see how shiny they were when you sold them on for a fiver? Did you notice that? Do you know why they were shiny? Because she handled them every day. They were all she had left of him. Photographs are no good to her, see. Bert he was called – he was hero, kid. He was a true fucking hero. And that fact makes you even more of a lowlife.

"You want to know how I know she'll pick you out?" Reg's top lip was raised in disgust, his massive hands curling into fists. "You smell like a sewer. That's how she described you to me. A sewer. And that's how I know it was you."

Grant backed up till the wall stopped him, and that was about the time I realised I was trapped with a knifeman and crazy fucker. Despite that, I couldn't stop myself saying, "Drop the knife, Grant."

Grant stared at Reg. "No fucking way, man."

"He's not going to touch you. Are you, Reg?"

Reg ignored me.

"Are you, Reg?"

"Tell me you did it."

"Reg, back off, leave him alone."

"I know you did it, kid. You just got to admit it."

"Reg," I warned. And then to the kid, "Did you do it?"

"Leave me alone."

"Did you do it?"

"Fuck you!"

"You tell me now, kid."

"No!"

"Did you fucking do it!"

"Yes," he whispered. "I did it."

Reg was about to lunge, "Stop," I shouted. "Reg, you will leave him alone. Do you *fucking* hear me!"

Reg didn't really get a chance to answer. The lift jerked, the lights flickered slightly and then we were moving again. Through the door's window, the bricks were tumbling quickly, becoming a blur. The old lift motor was whirring again, cables twanging in the lift shaft.

Grant nearly stumbled, and Reg took his chance, swiped aside the blade and threw a punch at Grant's face. If it had connected as intended, his head would have imploded like a crushed egg, but Grant moved just enough to make it a glancing blow, and the fist dented the steel wall.

I was about to scream at Grant to drop the knife when I saw him bring it up and saw it disappear inside Reg somewhere. It could have been his abdomen, I wasn't sure.

The lift stopped, the red numbers displayed 10 and my world had turned from boring to crazy into the space of a few short minutes. So crazy that I couldn't see straight, couldn't process the enormity of what the hell was happening in front of me. That though was partly because everything was so cramped. What with my kit at my feet and the lift only being five feet square, it was crowded, it was fast, hot and furious. And I missed it.

Reg grunted as the doors began to open, and for a second I thought he was going to collapse. Grant stood back to assess his handiwork.

"Grant," I said, "What the fuck…"

Grant turned to look at me just as Reg swung a mighty blow that connected well this time. And although my world had been frenzied over the last minute or so, all the rush fell away quite suddenly. I saw a tooth sail passed me so slowly I could have caught it, I saw a thin shower of blood speckle the air in front of my eyes before it patterned the lift wall, and I saw Grant's face become a rumpled and creased façade of agony before relaxing as his entire upper body sailed through the open door. His head hit the concrete and sounded like a well struck cricket ball heading for a six.

And then it was all quiet.

Reg doubled up and the packet of cigarettes fell out of his shirt pocket. There was redness in that shirt, lots of it, turning it shiny. His face twisted in pain, his reddened knuckles propping him against the floor. His breathing was fierce, ragged, and he looked at me, almost pleading. And I stood there like a numb fool.

I always said I was no hero, just an average arsehole, no pretender, what you see, blah blah.

I left the lift and stood over Grant. That's when I saw his eyes cloud over like they'd filled with milk from the inside. I even heard his final exhale. There were speckles of blood on his cheek, but that was about all. Any blood from the missing tooth was inside his closed mouth. But beneath his head more soaked into his hair. A one-punch kill.

Reg shuffled through the doorway and joined me, holding a hand over his belly, blood seeping out between his fingers and dripping onto the floor. He was gasping for breath, hyperventilating, and that's when I saw the look in his eyes, the steely resolution, the admission of being a killer, the *pride* he felt at killing a scrote, remorseless. "Self-defence." He staggered away towards 68.

"Reg. Get back here, I'm calling an ambulance."

He stopped. Eventually, he turned and staggered back to me. I could see the knife in his hand and I could see the look on his face. At first I didn't recognise it; I thought it was the pain that crumpled his face like that. I suppose it was, but it was the eyes – they'd changed, they'd become a killer's eyes. And now they were looking at me. And behind them was a killer's brain, and it was thinking like a killer; it was thinking things I shuddered to imagine. If I thought this horror movie had died when Grant did, I was wrong. And I almost couldn't believe it.

"Stay put, Reg, till I've got the cavalry here. And an ambulance too. Okay?"

He shook his head. "No cavalry, Eddie. No ambulance."

"You taking the piss?"

"Deadly serious, mate," he said. "I'm walking away now. And you're going to say nothing. Right? That's how we work; you and me, it's how it's always been. Am I right?"

"Let me see. You're guilty of false imprisonment – you admitted dragging the kid here, remember. You're guilty of assault. And, this is the real doozy, you just killed the fucker, and you want me to what? Say he tripped? Or say I just found him like this?"

"You got it. That's exactly how you'll tell it." The knife in his hand jerked. "Isn't it?"

"Maybe if it was 1979, but things have moved on. I don't give a shit if you were once a copper, I don't give a shit if you were head of Scotland fucking Yard, you ain't moving till CID gets here."

"They'll lock me up, and I can't let that happen."

"They don't beat the shit out of people these days. You've got nothing to worry about. Self-defence, remember?"

This didn't really impress Reg too much. The knife, rather than being a something timid and shy, twitching down the side of his leg, almost benign, suddenly became the centre of attention, shouting at me, getting in my face, threatening me.

Threatening me.

There's one thing a potential enemy should always know about me: never threaten me. Ever. "Reg—"

The knife lunged and if I'd been a bit slower, if I'd not had that last coffee before I left home, the blade would have been somewhere inside my right eye by now. He was injured and he was a pensioner, but Reg moved like a greased whippet and what little bravado I'd displayed for his benefit pissed its pants and ran away. "Whoa, Reg, you drop that sodding knife now before—"

This time it slashed, its tip missed my throat by about the same distance as my supervisor's stapler had missed my head this morning. Now I was panicking. I had nowhere to go, except back inside the lift, and that would have been the end of me.

We were facing each other, padding our feet like a couple of slim sumo wrestlers, and I had the feeling that Reg was enjoying this. I also had another, more sombre feeling. This was Reg's swan song – the old saying 'You'll never take me alive, copper' bounced around my head and so did an image of Butch Cassidy and The Sundance Kid rushing into a hail of Mexican gunfire. It would have been funny if I'd had a sense of humour.

I did what I had to do. I slid the eighteen inch Maglite from its loop on my belt. Reg nodded solemnly and came at me hard. He swung the blade, missed by a yard, and I swung the Mag upwards right into his chin. His head flipped backwards, he grunted and then hit the deck next to Grant's body, the knife by his side.

It was only then I remembered to press the panic button on my radio. It breaks through all transmissions, sends a bleeping out to all radios and opens the mic so you can shout your address and status. All I wanted to shout was, 'Bring coffee. And Whisky!'

The first of them took about three minutes to arrive.

CID showed up while I was half way through my second cigarette. When they asked what had happened, I handed them my mobile phone. "I recorded it all." And then I looked at Reg, "Old coppers never die, they just get twisted."

About the author:

Andrew Barrett is a crime and thriller writer based in Wakefield (England). He has been writing since the early 1990s, has completed several novels, and co-written a number of television scripts.

Andrew's work crosses a number of subject areas while maintaining his focus on the world of Crime Scene Investigators. He offers a unique insight into this often dark landscape, making good use of his 19 years' professional expertise as a crime scene examiner to envelop the reader in exciting yet realistic thrillers.

To find out more, please visit:

www.andrew-barrett.co.uk

Books by Andrew Barrett:

A Long Time Dead	Roger Conniston book 1
Stealing Elgar	Roger Conniston book 2
No More Tears	Roger Conniston book 3
The Third Rule	Eddie Collins book 1
Black by Rose	Eddie Collins book 2
The Lift	Eddie Collins short story 1
Sword of Damocles	Eddie Collins book 3

Made in the USA
Charleston, SC
09 February 2016